GOLDEN RULES

Wit and Wisdom of
The Golden Girls

BY FRANCESCO SEDITA AND DOUGLAS YACKA

Penguin Workshop

To Sue and Danielle. And many years
of cheesecake—FS & DY

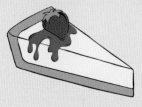

PENGUIN WORKSHOP
An Imprint of Penguin Random House LLC, New York

©ABC Studios. © 2019 Disney Enterprises, Inc. Published by Penguin Workshop, an imprint of Penguin Random House LLC, New York. PENGUIN and PENGUIN WORKSHOP are trademarks of Penguin Books Ltd, and the W colophon is a registered trademark of Penguin Random House LLC. Manufactured in China.

Visit us online at www.penguinrandomhouse.com.

ISBN 9781524792114   10 9 8 7 6 5 4 3 2 1

Picture it . . .

Blanche: What was your first impression of me?

Rose: I thought you wore too much makeup and were a slut. I was wrong. You don't wear too much makeup.

Is it possible to love two men at the same time?

Set the scene—have we been drinking?

Dorothy: I have a date.

Blanche: With a man?

Dorothy: No, Blanche, with a Venus flytrap!

Rose, I have to confess, I dabbled a little in poetry writing in high school.

That's nothing to be ashamed of. A lot of tall girls who wouldn't get dates wrote poetry in high school.

My mother survived a slight stroke, which left her, if I can be frank . . . a complete burden.

Sticks and
stones can
break your
bones, but
cement pays
homage to
tradition.

Blanche: Well, what do you know, Sophia has a past!

Sophia: That's right, but unlike yours, I didn't need penicillin to get through it.

I have been told I bear a striking resemblance to Miss Cheryl Ladd . . . although my bosoms are perkier.

Not even if you were hanging upside down on a trapeze!

Dorothy: Oh, like you never told a lie?

Rose: That's right, I've never told a lie. Well, just once, when I snuck out of class to go to the movies.

Dorothy: That's not much of a lie.

Rose: That's what I thought. Turned out to be the day they taught EVERYTHING!

Dorothy: The final piece of the puzzle.

You won't believe the horrible thing I just heard on the radio!

Oh, Rose, we go through this every time. *This is merely a test. In the event of an actual emergency . . .*

Have I given you any indication at all that I care?

Ninety-eight pounds. I can't remember the last time I weighed ninety-eight. Probably college.

Where'd you go to college, Blanche? The University of Jupiter?

I take very good care of myself. I treat my body like a temple.

Yeah, open to everyone, day or night.

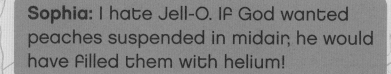

Sophia: I hate Jell-O. If God wanted peaches suspended in midair, he would have filled them with helium!

Rose: My mother always used to say, *The older you get, the better you get, unless you're a banana.*

Let's rent an adult video, drink mimosas, and French-kiss the pillows.

Can I ask a dumb question?

Better than anyone I know.

I would kill Gloria if she ever wrote about my sexual escapades!

My name
is Blanche
Devereaux.
That's French
for Blanche
Devereaux.

Now, if you'll excuse me, I'm gonna go take a long, hot, steamy bath with just enough water to barely cover my perky bosoms.

You're only gonna sit in an inch of water?!

Blanche: Dorothy, do you realize it has been four days since I have enjoyed the company of a man?
Dorothy: I know, Blanche, I've been marking the days off on my "Big Ships of the Navy" calendar.

We were never allowed
to wear berets when
I was in high school.
It was against the
St. Olaf dress code.
They did let me wear
a paper cap a lot.
It was long and pointy.

Sophia: I always wondered why blessings wore disguises. If I were a blessing, I'd run around naked.

Rose: I just wish my mother and father were here to see this.

Blanche: Because they'd be so proud of you?

Rose: No, because they'd be alive.

May you put
your dentures
in upside down
and chew your
head off!

I could have been living in a swinging condo, instead of with—I better not say anything until I've had my coffee . . .

... a slut and a moron!

There is a thin line between having a good time and becoming an obvious wanton slut. I know. My toe has been on that line.

No offense, Dorothy, but your cupcakes are dry and tasteless. Nobody ever likes your cupcakes.

My cupcakes are moist and delicious. Men *love* my cupcakes.

Rose: I'll get the cheesecake.

Blanche: I'll get the whipped cream.

Dorothy: I'll get the chocolate syrup.

Sophia: I'll get the Polaroid, this is a time to remember!

Dorothy: Ma, you don't have a Polaroid.

Blanche: I'll get mine! It's under my bed. I have to go in there for the whipped cream anyway . . .

Thank you for being a friend.